sammy goes to speech

written by marissa siegel
illustrated by kat taylor

I'm Sammy. I'm three years old.

I think someone took my voice!

Mommy comes in every morning to wake me up.
She tickles me until I giggle!

I want to tell her so much, but I can't.

"Where is your voice?" "Who took it?"

I try to say "it's right here!"

All that comes out is air.
I really,

really want to talk.

"Let's go find your voice!"

we look under the bed.

"IS your voice under here?"

Nope! It iSN't there!

We look in the closet.

"Is your voice in here?"

It's not here either!

"Did maggie lick it and accidentally swallow it? Silly maggie!"

I think my voice might be gone forever.

"we've just got to find that voice!"

The next day mommy and I go to see Miss Hunter.

I get to play with toys in the waiting room.

We go to Miss Hunter's room.
We make silly faces!

"We are going to find your voice, Sammy!"

Miss Hunter shows me how to make a big mouth "ah" sound.

We use our hands and our mouths.

I say,

"ah!"

Miss Hunter helps me put my lips together to make the

MM MM YUM
M sound.

I can do it! I feed Mr. Monster.
He likes snacks!

MM MM YUM!

My voice was at speech the whole time!
Miss Hunter helps me find it
each time I go to speech.

Mommy is so happy when I use my voice.
She learns new ways to play
and practice with me.
I get high fives and stickers too!

At home, we say words back and forth.
we laugh and play!

At snack time, I say more and please.

At bed time, I say night night. we all say I love you, even mr. monster and maggie.

Now I say what I want and I say what I see. I say NO NO NO and I say I'm three!

We hope you have enjoyed Sammy Goes to Speech! This book is intended to be read for fun as well as to be used as an educational tool by parents, educators, and speech-language pathologists.

Tips

1. If you think your child is experiencing difficulties with his or her communication, seek out a professional such as a licensed speech-language pathologist (SLP). An SLP can help you determine if your child requires an evaluation.

2. There are many ways to help children with speech delays and disorders. Only a few of the techniques are showcased in this book and may or may not be the best choice for your child.

3. Family members, speech-language pathologists, and educators are a big part of your child's speech team and there are things you can all do right now to improve your child's communication skills!

Activities to Develop Your Child's Communication Skills

1. Talk about what your child is doing. You can think of it as narrating their day. Research has shown that the more words your child hears, the better their communication skills, and even academic skills later on.

2. Build and expand on what your child says. If he or she says "more," you can say "You want more. You want more crackers. These are yummy crackers."

3. Encourage imitation and turn-taking games, especially those that incorporate movement of the hands and mouth.

4. Sing songs together. Nursery rhymes are perfect for this.

5. Visit a new place as a vocabulary-building adventure. Take your time to talk about the things you see and point them out. Try to use as many senses as you can. Look, listen, smell, and touch!

6. Use speech and language that is clear and simple as a model for your child. Reinforce all attempts to speak. You can encourage attempts by speaking back and showing joint attention.

7. Read books together! Books can be useful tools in creating meaningful communication. Whether it be pointing at pictures together, attempting repetitive phrases found on each page, or even asking and answering a variety of questions, there are many ways to combine communication development with books.

If you have any questions, contact your pediatrician or licensed speech-language pathologist.

A percentage of the proceeds from this book will go to supporting efforts in the research of communication sciences and disorders.

Made in the USA
Lexington, KY
10 November 2019